Be An Expert!™

Seasons

Erin Kelly

Children's Press®
An imprint of Scholastic Inc.

Contents

Welcome, Spring! 4

Spring Is Fun! ....

Know the Names

Be an expert! Get to know the four seasons.

Welcome, Fall! ....

Winter Is Fun! 1

2

lcome, Summer!...8

Summer Is Fun!..........10

ll Is Fun!................14

Welcome, Winter!........16

the Seasons......20

Expert Quiz........................21
Expert Gear.......................22
Glossary............................23
Index.................................24

Welcome, Spring!

The days are warm. Flowers **bloom**.

Expert Fact

Many baby animals are born in spring. There is a lot of food to eat, and the **weather** is warm.

Spring Is Fun!

Some days are rainy. After a spring shower, you can jump in a puddle!

Zoom In

Find this spring gear in the big picture.

umbrella   raincoat   rain boots   rain hat

Welcome, Summer!

Days can be hot and sunny! The sunshine helps plants grow.

Signs of the Season

Q: What do adult birds do in summer?

A: They help their babies learn to fly, find food, and stay safe.

Summer Is Fun!

There are many ways to stay cool. You can go for a swim!

Zoom In

Find this summer gear in the big picture.

sunblock • swim goggles • flip-flops • sunglasses

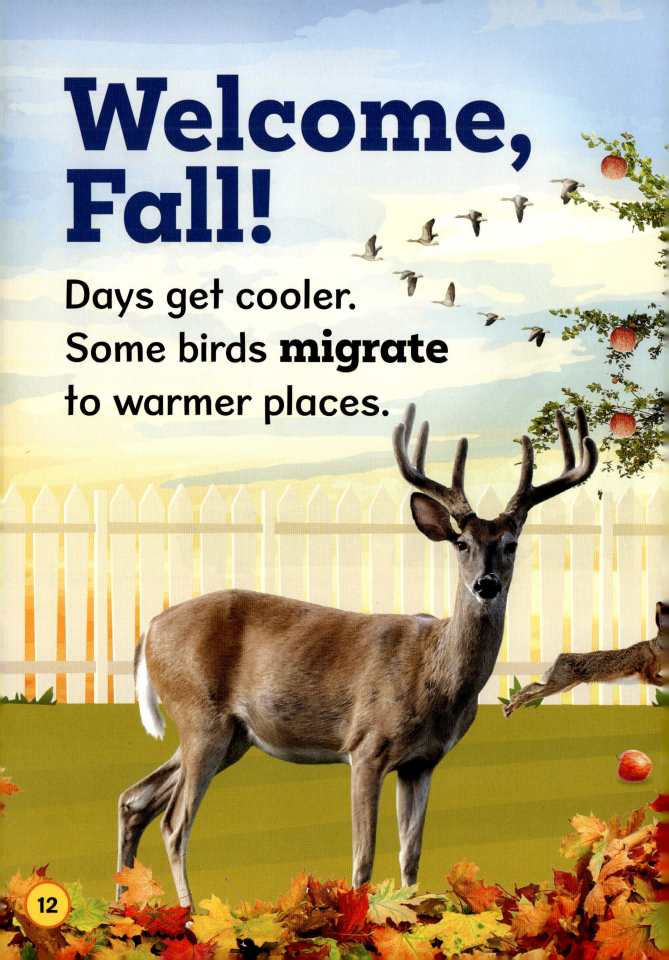

Welcome, Fall!

Days get cooler. Some birds **migrate** to warmer places.

Expert Fact

Deciduous (di-SIJ-oo-uhs) trees lose their leaves in fall. Evergreen trees keep their leaves or needles all year long.

Fall Is Fun!

You can pick some apples! Then jump in a pile of leaves.

Zoom In

Find this fall gear in the big picture.

| vest | long pants | long sleeves | sweater |

Welcome, Winter!

It is cold!
Snow is falling.

Signs of the Season

Q: Can animals find food in winter?

A: It can be hard. That is why some animals eat a lot in fall to put on weight. In winter, they **hibernate**.

Winter Is Fun!

Bundle up! You can make a snowman or go sledding!

Zoom In

Find this winter gear in the big picture.

| hat | glove | coat | earmuffs |

All the Seasons

Nature changes with the seasons. And they are so much fun!

1.

2.

5.

6.

Expert Quiz

Can you name the season when these things can happen? Then you are an expert! See if someone else can be an expert too!

4.

8.

Answers: 1. Winter, 2. Spring, 3. Fall, 4. Summer, 5. Summer, 6. Winter, 7. Spring, 8. Fall.

Glossary

bloom (BLOOM): to produce flowers or to be in flower.

hibernate (HYE-bur-nate): to spend the winter sleeping or resting.

migrate (MYE-grate): to move to another area or climate at a particular time of year.

weather (WETH-ur): the condition of the outside air at a particular time and place. In winter, the weather is often cold.

Index

animals 4, 17

apples 14

binoculars...............22

birds......................9, 12

boots 22

fall.......................12–15

fall gear 15

first aid kit.............22

flowers...............4, 23

food..................4, 9, 17

hibernate...........17, 23

leaves..................13, 14

migrate 12, 23

nature guide...........22

plants 8

puddle 6

snow.........................16

spring....................4–7

spring gear..............7

summer...............8–11

summer gear 11

sun.............................8

trees 13

water bottle 22

weather 4, 6, 8, 12, 16, 23

winter.................16–19

winter gear.............19

|||||||||||||||||||||||||||||||||||||||||||||||||||||||||||||||||||||||||||||||||

Library of Congress Cataloging-in-Publication Data
    Names: Kelly, Erin Suzanne, 1965– author.
Title: Seasons/by Erin Kelly.
Other titles: Be an expert! (Scholastic Inc.)
Description: Book edition. | New York: Children's Press, an imprint of Scholastic Inc., 2022. | Series: Be an expert | Includes index. | Audience: Ages 3–5. | Audience: Grades K–1. | Summary: "One season is hot. One season is cold. The others are a little bit in-between! What do you know about the seasons? With this book, you can become an expert! Feel like a pro with exciting photos, expert facts, and fun challenges. Can you name which season is good for swimming and which is good for sledding? Try it! Then see if you can pass the Expert Quiz!"—Provided by publisher.
Identifiers: LCCN 2021025669 (print) | LCCN 2021025670 (ebook) | ISBN 9781338798067 (library binding) | ISBN 9781338798074 (paperback) | ISBN 9781338798081 (ebk)
Subjects: LCSH: Seasons—Juvenile literature.
Classification: LCC QB637.4.K458 2022 (print) | LCC QB637.4 (ebook) | DDC 508.2—dc23
LC record available at https://lccn.loc.gov/2021025669
LC ebook record available at https://lccn.loc.gov/2021025670

Copyright © 2022 by Scholastic Inc.

All rights reserved. Published by Children's Press, an imprint of Scholastic Inc., *Publishers since 1920*. SCHOLASTIC, CHILDREN'S PRESS, BE AN EXPERT!™, and associated logos are trademarks and/or registered trademarks of Scholastic Inc.

The publisher does not have any control over and does not assume any responsibility for author or third-party websites or their content.

No part of this publication may be reproduced, stored in a retrieval system, or transmitted in any form or by any means, electronic, mechanical, photocopying, recording, or otherwise, without written permission of the publisher. For information regarding permission, write to Scholastic Inc., Attention: Permissions Department, 557 Broadway, New York, NY 10012.

10 9 8 7 6 5 4 3 2 1   22 23 24 25 26

Printed in Heshan, China 62
First edition, 2022

Series produced by Spooky Cheetah Press
Design by The Design Lab, Kathleen Petelinsek
Cover design by Three Dogs Design LLC

Photos ©: cover top and throughout: skynesher/Getty Images; back cover center: Richard Nelson/Dreamstime; cover main: Ryan Etter; 1 top left and throughout: Alexander Potapov/Dreamstime; 2 bottom right: Ariel Skelley/Getty Images; 3 top right boy: anirav/Getty Images; 3 top right girl: mdmilliman/Getty Images; 3 center left boy: RichLegg/Getty Images; 3 center left girl: LWA/Dann Tardif/Getty Images; 5 top right tree: Steve Callah Dreamstime; 9 top right tree: K Quinn Ferris/Dreamstime; 9 right inset: Nicola Gavin/Alamy Images; 10-11 pool: filipok/Getty Images; 15 inset top: sam74100/Getty Images; 16 center: CoreyFord/Getty Images; 17 inset top: DenKuvaiev/Getty Images; 19 bottom right: LWA/Dann Tardif/Getty Image 19 bottom left: Ariel Skelley/Getty Images; 20 bottom right: Ariel Skelley/Getty Images; 22 hiker: Austinadams/Dreamstime.

All other photos © Shutterstock.